This story is a personal one. I am a children's writer and illustrator and I have MS. I decided to put down my own experiences but through my son's eyes. It is a work of fiction in that sense but based on events that occured in my life. As my son has got older he has started to ask more about what MS is, I thought that this book would help explain things in a really mild way. And to share it, thinking that some other people with MS (or loved ones of people with MS) and children might find it useful.

Any view points are my own and I am not a medical expert.
I have gathered the factology from Wikipedia and the MS Society, as of October 2019.
I would like to say thank you to all the people who have been a huge support to me.
Mostly my fantastic family. My most wonderful husband, two amazing children and my parents.
A special thanks to the nurse at RVI Newcastle Upon Tyne who ran after me after my diagnosis to offer support in July 2014.
and Dr. G. Davies, for amazing support and help. And the staff at BrAMS

A GUIDE TO MULTIPLE SCLEROSIS FOR CHILDREN

MUMMY'S GOT MS

BY CHARITY RUSSELL

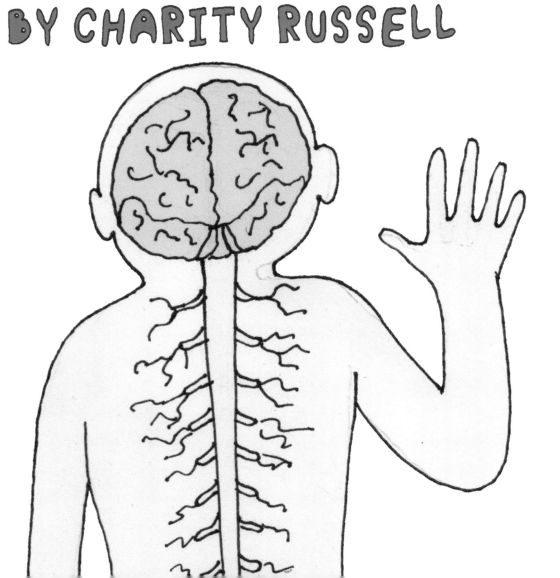

Together we went into a big machine (because I was in her tummy). It made such a noise! It banged and it whirred and the radiologist took pictures of mummy on the inside.

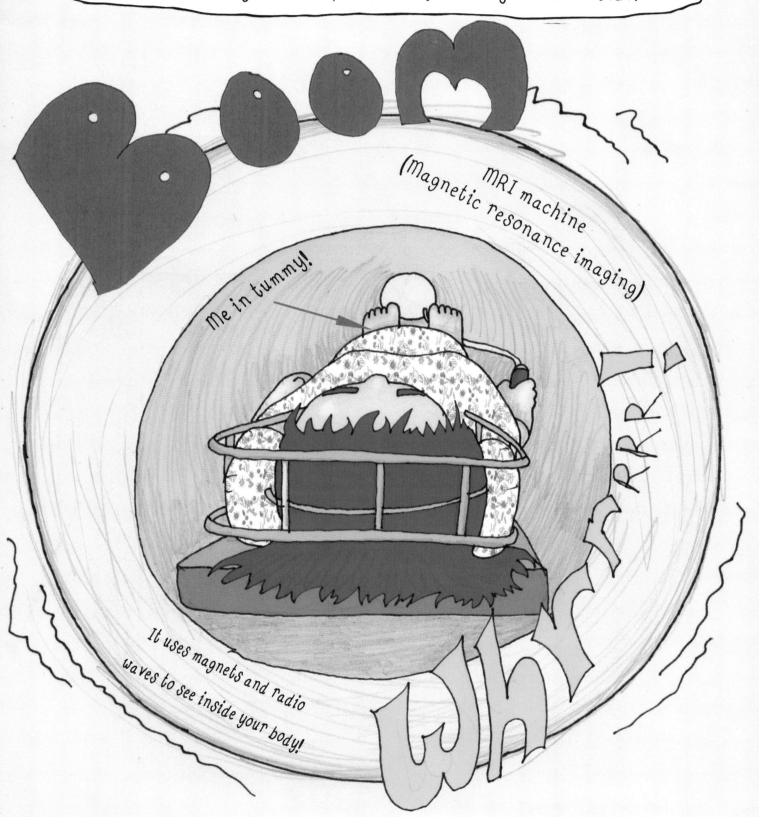

Then I was born and she started to get better.
But one day she got a numb spot on her leg
and it spread and spread and spread,
and this time spread a little bit more.
I went with mummy to lots of appointments,
She went into the whirry machine (I waited outside).
She saw doctors and more doctors.
I was with her when they told her that she had
something called MS.

Mummy sometimes would use a stick. It helped her balance, it also helped tell other people that they should be patient with her speed!

Sometimes mummy found it difficult to walk.
It would take us ages to get anywhere.
I didn't mind, it gave me the chance to
balance along walls and practice walking without
touching any paving cracks.

When I started school, I worried that she had to go
to all the appointments on her own.
But she didn't need to go so much anymore.
She did injections three times a week and they helped loads!

The MS affected mummy's speach too, her actual words!
One day she said, "Wow! Look at that beautiful umbrella."
She was pointing at a rainbow.

There are lots of people who help my mummy.
Neurologists, nurses, phlebotomists, scientists,
charities, my daddy, my sister, my Ouma and Oupa.
And of course ME!

WHAT IS MS?

MS is short for Multiple Sclerosis. It is Latin and means Lots of scars.

Brain

Spinal Cord

The nervous system is the brain, spinal cord and all the nerves.

MYELITIS is inflammation of the spinal cord which can disrupt the normal responses from the brain to the rest of the body, and from the rest of the body to the brain.

A Nerve

Healthy

Damaged

In MS, the myelin covering nerve fibers in the brain and spinal cord becomes damaged, slowing or blocking electrical signals from reaching the eyes, muscles and other parts of the body.

The nervous system is the brain, spinal cord and all the nerves. Everything in our body is controlled by the nervous system. So if part of it get's damaged the communication between the brain and that part of the body can become muddled or lost.

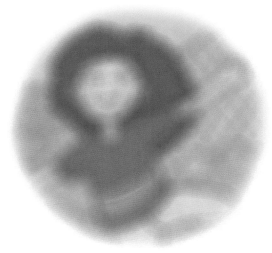

Normal Sight

Sight with Nerve damage

For Example; Someone with MS may have problems seeing, that is because the eye has a big nerve called the optic nerve which has been damaged.

There are special medicines called DMD **(Disease Modifying Drugs)**
That patients can take.
Some are tablets, some are injections and some are infusions
(when the patient goes to the hospital
and the medicine is put into their body over several hours).
People with MS are affected differently.

PEOPLE WHO HELP MUMMY

A RADIOLOGIST
A doctor who is specially trained to interpret diagnostic images such as X-rays, MRI and CT scans.

There are lots of Support places online.

All the people that raise money and awareness by running or baking or simply chatting or not chatting- my sister once did a sponsored silence to raise funds to support an MS group!

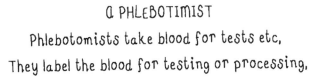

A PHLEBOTIMIST

Phlebotomists take blood for tests etc,
They label the blood for testing or processing,
and enter patient information into a database.
They assemble and maintain medical instruments
such as needles, test tubes, and blood vials.
They take my mummy's blood to make sure the
medicine she takes isn't causing harm.

A NURSE

Mummy's hospital have a unit
of special MS nurses.
She can phone their helpline
when she has
symptoms or worries about
MS.

A SCIENTIST

The scientists work in a laboratory,
searching for treatment, cures and the
Whats, Wheres And Whys.

A NEUROLOGIST

The neurologist treats disorders that affect
the brain, spinal cord, and nerves.